THESE SHOES

FLOW AND THOUGHTS BY

ERIK MOTON

PUBLISHED BY FIDELI PUBLISHING INC.

THESE SHOES

ISBN: 978-1-60414-913-5

Published by:

Fideli Publishing Inc.
119 W. Morgan St.
Martinsville, IN 46151

www.FideliPublishing.com

These Shoes

Maybe the image would be clearer
if you step in front of a mirror,
but don't stare too long
because your reflection may not know the song
of someone's highs versus their lows.
Try them on and see how it goes.
Tie up the laces then admit
what you thought you knew is not a perfect fit

ME,
THE BEGINNINGS

Contents

A Little Black Boy

A little black boy is in a wheelchair.
He does not know why people stop and stare.

Maybe they think he has no mind of his own,
but give him a textbook and it will be shown.

He always knew he was smart,
and he kept that thought in his heart.

He'll always hope, pray, and hold on tight.
Before you know it, he'll be walking in everyone's sight.

But, some people say that he'll never walk again,
but he refuses to let the devil win.

This little black boy has a smart mind.
Him and I are two of a kind.

We keep our dreams together,
but his dreams will last forever.

So, as you can see
this little black boy is me
having this big catastrophe.

But, I have what I need to go on and succeed
with my great deed.

I'm not going to let anyone pull me down
until I rot and turn crispy brown.

I'm going to fight until the time is right.
I'm going to get up and walk one day
having it my own special way.

Remember, don't forget the little black boy
because he is not a boy toy.
He is me, your friend, as you can see.

It's Just Me

Sometimes I explode in a moment of sexual heat
like an untamed lion refusing to keep his seat
at a young age I was taunted with suicidal suggestions
but I chose to lift my head above the world's aggression
it's just my expression to leave this earth with a good impression
I choose to be a spiritual being
no matter what, I can't be sidetracked by the unforeseen
I'll give my right arm to a dedication
I give my heart in a crisis situation
the complication comes when I allow the world's makeup the
opportunity to seal my lips and shut me up
I had to give that certain behavior up and I broke the spell
I spoke my peace without having to raise hell
I've realized that no matter what I do people tell lies
but when it's all said and done they won't provide alibis
when I'm alone I dig through all my actions and pain
to see if this is the personality in which I should remain
I learned to look in the mirror and marvel at what I see
because deep down inside it's just *ME*

Mirror

Hello me, or is it hello you?
I can't really decipher the similar things we do.
I try to wash away the chemical makeup,
but the harder I scrub, the more I find your past, my present.
You seem to know what's next, so save me from myself.

Mirror, yesterday I cracked you with my discontentment,
but I was forced to heal my wounds. I can't pretend I don't need
you in my life.
Mirror, I loved you today. You reflected my realities, good and bad.
You reminded me to live the fun I've always wished I had...

Why I Hold It All Inside

The strangest feeling has invaded me
Too much drama in this society
A certain image I am to maintain
Open to stability
Immune to change
All the tears I've shed have been dried
But why do I choose to hold it all inside

My premonitions are revealed to be quite real
Which tend to ignite my concerns and dampen my thrill
A few times I believed I was in love
But held it inside because I felt I wasn't deserving of
Now I know better and I don't hide
I wish there were some in whom I can confide
Still the question remains why do I hold it all inside

I hold it all inside because no matter how I feel
I tend to trade my emotions for the unreal
I hold it all inside because there are times I feel I'm on my own
I hold it all inside to have something to hold on to when I'm alone
I hold it all inside because people have their own issues to go through
I hold it all inside because you don't believe me
    when I tell you that it's true

Who I Am

The moon is dark and parts of the world are damned
The sun ceases to shine, but I'm determined to remember who I am
I'm not the type of person you see cruising the streets
I'm not the type who celebrates in time of defeat
I'm not the type who associates with drugs
I'm not the one going around claiming to be a thug
I'm the type of person who stares the phrase "can't do" in the face
The one who speaks his mind, and doesn't feel out of place
I'm the type who holds his head up high,
And the one who is not satisfied with just getting by
I'm the one who lets words of discouragement remain mute to the ear
The one who doesn't forget that God is here
I'm the type that finds good in every bad
The one who realizes there's no sense in being sad
I'm the type of person who doesn't care to be someone else
I'm the STRONG BLACK MAN that finds GREAT HAPPINESS in self

Easy Life

If life was easy I wouldn't experience growth. Instead, I would lavish in the simple and reject the complex. If life was easy I would be weak minded and often reminded hard work is a myth. If life was easy thoughts would harmonize causing folks not to realize it's essential to disagree. If life was easy challenges would decay. If life was easy why need a brighter day?

Me

I look into your eyes, and what do I see?
A joyous, happier version of me
I look into the future, and what do I find?
A caring, respectful friend I can call mine
I search my heart, and what do I come across?
All the smiles and other things that I thought were lost
I open my mouth, and what do I say?
Obviously, all the wrong things to send you astray
I lend my ears, and what do you have to say?
Evidently, all the right things to take the pain away
I breathe, and what does that prove?
That I'm human and not too proud to step into the groove
I wonder, and what's the punishment?
The world's shock and astonishment
I learn to love, and what's my surprise?
No more lonely tears exit my eyes
I step into reality, and what's proven to be true?
God blessed me with the strength to do the same or more as you
I observe my surroundings to solve the mystery
as to why the *you* wants to discredit *ME*

My Worth

Speculated rumors about us
How long will we let them humor us?
You're worth it
How about me?

MYSELF AND I

Visions

Good morning
I awoke feeling short changed, estranged
from the one I thought would provide protection from rejection,
so I decided to rearrange the strange vision that I had of you
being my joy and comfort, my all and all.
I shouldn't have to remind you that a relationship equals two;
a version of me, a sample of you.
It's crazy that my vision is hazy.

Good afternoon
I went out with someone I haven't seen in a long time
and with him I could be honest and speak my mind.
I breathed him, I kissed him, I hugged him most importantly,
I loved him. This person is the reflection that I see.
I thank God for this person he gave me, Me.
I shouldn't have to remind you that a relationship equals two;
an acknowledgement of me, instead of always focusing on you.
It's crazy that my vision remains hazy.

Good evening
I spent time gathering my thoughts,
and wondered why in your life I'm an afterthought.
You have to squeeze in time instead of having me already on your list.
Don't rejoice because I'm not pissed.
See, I know that life goes on and the sun continues to shine.
I shouldn't have to remind you that a relationship equals two;
a love of me, instead of an infatuation of you.
I admit today that it's crazy that my vision still remains hazy.

Yesterday's Promise

Yesterday, the promise was ripe like a sweet, smelling Georgia peach, expectation loomed, and the day continued with ease. My self-esteem rose like a sunrise's greeting. There was no cause for doubt.

Today, the promise is a dried, decaying image, lingering still, but not at a high capacity. If I make it to the end of the day, it will greet me like a constant regret. My facial expression will be cold as stone. There will be doubt at high magnitudes.

It would've been nice if only truth had had the upper hand.

Trust

How do I go about accomplishing you? I thought I embodied you in my arms, but that "special" someone believed me to be a fake. You are so easy to speak, yet your meaning deepens the simple and meek. Can you, will you, give me another chance?

Chance

Comes once in a lifetime
Perhaps more if people would relax their mind
Momentarily, puts dreamers in the driver's seat
Suddenly, allows fantasies to become quick moments of heat
Passes you by in a glance
Leaves you hopeless as a victim of circumstance

Circumstance

Victimizes even the best of the best
Corners you against a wall to see if you can pass the test
Gives you few options, but you do what you must to try
to figure out whom in this situation you can trust

Goodbye Infatuation

Goodbye Infatuation
thanks for leading me to fake admiration...
thanks for showing me that I was a fool in love
with the possibility of falling in love with that special one...
The pain you've caused is in desperate need of care

Goodbye Infatuation
thanks for having that person look completely over me,
and right through me like I had been sprayed with Windex...
thanks for lighting a flame to a fire that was never meant to burn,
and forgetting to teach me the lesson that I was to learn

Goodbye Infatuation
thanks for killing the theory of love at first sight,
and allowing me to question real love...
thanks for being by my side when I wished upon a star,
only to have my wish come laugh in my face

Goodbye Infatuation
thanks for enabling me not to miss you...
thanks for the hurtful experience of knowing the truth...
thanks for taking me on a road to nowhere...
now, you can leave just like you entered, on time, but in a hurry

Why I Started Writing Poetry

I needed to get something off my mind
so I picked up a pencil and started to rhyme
I got so involved I lost track of time
I didn't realize I left the past behind

I wanted you to know how I felt about you
so I found something creative to do
and then discovered a dream for me to pursue
It really kept me from being blue
then it helped me stay true about the situations I was going through
It enabled me to accept my natural hue
and gave me strength to start my life anew

Some may choose not to give a damn
that I write about such things like who I am
but I wanted to do me so I started writing poetry

Still, I Cry Alone @ Night

I have many associates that I truly believe don't mean me any harm,
but whenever trouble lurks, they disappear at the sound of my alarm.
They swear by the moon that they love me.
As long as I have money, there's no other place they would rather be.
I choose to be peaceful and not argue and fight.
I think that's being respectful....still, I cry alone at night.

Promises, promises that they couldn't keep.
I still have to be forgiving and not lose any sleep.
I try to give them what they perspire out,
but then recant because that's not what I'm about.
I'm still living, still in sight.
I become lost in the crowd....still, I cry alone at night.

You think I want your pity, or what I say is not true?
Well, take a look in the mirror;
     there's a chance that who I'm speaking of is you.
I decided to welcome you from the darkness into the light.
Now, you're enlightened....still, I'll cry alone tonight.

Know Me

I am who I am and may forever be. You choose to pass me by without knowing who you see. I may not be able to get around like you and all the rest. You don't give me credit, but I may prove to be better than all the best. You think I'm crazy when you see me posting. Well, I'm an achiever. I don't believe in boasting. You say the negative when you honestly don't know. I'm on a mission. My life is not up for show. My skin is mahogany tone, my eyes a texture of brown. My self-confidence is astounding, so maybe that's why you try to bring me down. Despite what you have to say, I'm here as long as God see fit for me to stay. You only go by what you think you see, as time goes by without you knowing me.

Dear Heart

Lead me to find oneness with myself
Allow me to breathe a second of my own breath
Listening to you has gotten me shitted on time and time again
You took those people in even if I didn't want them as friends
So what if you've been broken countless times
Maybe you wouldn't be alone if you said what's on your mind
I tried to warn you your concern would seclude you
Now, their plans don't include you
If you were not around then I could be thoughtless,
    but you stay around
Oh how I wish I would've never sought this
because now I experience emptiness

Emptiness

A prolonged soul piercing
A hollow song
A desire for feeling that one belongs

Send Me Away

Put me in an envelope
Seal me with a kiss
Mail me to a place unlike this
I can't stand the hurt, the hatred is insane
I want to know Happiness, get to know her name
      But, I know you, so
Put me in a box
Stamp me with regret
Mark pity on me
Hate the day we met
Don't put the proper postage
Put me on the shelf
Leave me in this hell altogether
Move on to someone else

Breeze

You blow against me gently
with your soothing honey suckle skin.
I can close my eyes and for a few
feel that the world is mine.
You satisfy my needs beyond measures.

My Shell

My shell is where I dwell to remain
wholesome and well. There is enough
space to breathe and for me to temporarily receive
the Creator's shelter and His voice needed to survive.
I keep quiet and avoid the nonsense. What fun is it if
I can't keep them in suspense?

Sitting Here

The room is dimly lit
The television is on mute
Seclusion was my goal
Just to find my best attribute
Too many worries on my mind
I would like to address them all
But there seems not to be enough time

Sitting here all alone
True friends have come and gone
But from what I've learned
The sun will continue to shine
I must know that happiness is mine
To have and hold
Someday the truth will be told
And the puzzle will unfold
But until then I must love me forever and always

Sitting here now and again
With my thoughts blowing in the wind
I know that I'll succeed
My wants don't exceed my needs
But I feel there should be something more

Sitting here tomorrow and today
Waiting to embrace the better day
Will it come, or is it already here
I guess I can dry my tears
While I sit here

INSPIRATIONAL

Get On Up Child

Get on up, child, get on up
God didn't bring us this far to give us up
Take it from me this situation is not where I want to be,
But see I know God has plans for me
Whatever He choose to do
I have Faith that He'll bring me through
Get on up, child, get on up
It's pass time to put that smile on your face
Because God's Amazing Grace
Said "I once was lost, but now I'm found"
God's everlasting love
Oh, how I love that sound
Get on up, child, get on up
Don't deny His love and care
Although we forget, He's always there
To provide us with whatever we need
It's not much to ask for us to spiritually heed
Get on up, child , get on up
God doesn't need us stressing
He sends us an everyday blessing
Most of us get another chance to see another day
In which we can repent and pray
Tough times don't last long
They're just a test to see if we'll remain spiritually strong
In His word that is
Because everything here is already His
Get on up, child, get on up

Love is God and God is love
Oh, what a privilege it is to be invited to Heaven above
Get on up, child, get on up
Whatever His plans are doesn't have to be our mystery
What a blessing it is to give Him the victory
Yes, sometimes we have to cry,
But that doesn't mean we have to give up and spiritually die
So, get on up child, get on up
Get on up, child and keep your head up

Silence

Darkness has cast its spell over the house. Hesitating, I roll into your room. Usually, there are shards of uneasy thoughts, words thundering disappointment. Have recent events distanced us further?

Seeing your big, glowing eyes, I sense you will lash out at me. But you smile, reach out your hand. The arguing has found its peace. I sigh, roll closer. Together, we stare out into the calmness of silence.

Destiny

oblivious to life's calling
I sit back and relax,
  Breathe,
    then relax again
the unseen road,
    the darken path
      is no threat to me
it just has me wondering
      what's next
you come to me
    welcomed with opened arms,
and I'm more than ready to fulfill my Destiny
Destiny that gives me Purpose,
          Meaning,
          Life,
another chance to Live to complete my Destiny
  that I cannot change

Nobody is Perfect

Perfection:
The general rule of law
that opens up to a world of deception.
Trust is laid upon shaky grounds,
but then again reconsidered because
nobody is perfect.
Harmonizing pain and heartaches put to the side
making it easier to forgive because
nobody is perfect.
Mistakes are made,
but are they really if nobody is perfect?
Pleasing comfort in second and everlasting chances,
free to live in damning circumstances because
nobody is perfect.
Should it be considered a joke because anyone can be easily provoked?
Why put up the fuss if
nobody is perfect?
Is there perfect love? Perfect trust? Perfect stability? Perfect lust?
Perfect people? Perfect minds? Perfect beliefs? Perfect times?
Societal disorganization only because some are
chasing an unreachable world of
Perfection.

Comparison

Like the dawning sun, I rise
Like a warming hello, I smile
Like a caring person, I'm willing to go the extra mile
Like a bruised emotion, I hurt
Like a broken heart, I mend
Like a compassionate soul, I'm thoughtful of those I befriend
Like the river, I rage
Like the storm, I roar
Like a person who refuses to settle for less,
I'm searching for more
Like the wind, I refresh
Like a teacher, I teach
Like spoken words, there's a heart I'm trying to reach
Like a tree, I stand
Like the rain, I fall
Like a person built to endure, I put up with it all
Like a promise, I break
Like a vision, I inspire
Like a breezy wind, I remain cool
Even though folks keep adding fuel to the fire
Like ears, I listen
Like eyes, I see
Like serenity, I obtain wisdom to accept me

Pleasant Dreams

The world goes round and round
    with this being my second chance around
I believe that I'll be all that I was meant to be
The wind blows a chill against my head
I could think of the negativity, but then instead
I choose the pleasant dreams that sometimes seem
To come and then go again without me knowing
    when they'll come to an end
Someday it feels like I'll achieve and live outside my dreams

She's gone away, but she wasn't put here to stay
I try to look the other way, but the memories greet me the next day
When we meet again my heart will begin to mend,
    and we'll dance on the
Wind that brings us closer in
The pleasant dreams of tomorrow and all of the yesterdays
That were put on a pedestal and too soon drifted away
Time will tell of a sweet melody that captures all the dreams of me

We all have problems and must try to solve them
Before we lay heads to rest and emotions go unexpressed
Sometimes I doubt if mama and papa know best
I often wonder if life is a challenge of the best
To see if I have what it takes not to succumb
To sudden heartbreak and keep my head above all
That tends to make the sound of having the capability to
    bring me down
Life goes on and I know I will go on
My heart will continue to beat strong and I'm not on my own
The stars in the dark blue sky keeps me hoping for a try
As the moon beams down on my pleasant dreams

Zone One

That secret place visited frequently reserved for only one person to enter and only one to leave; a place to regroup and think about the choices made; where one can feel sheltered from the rain and only have their thoughts to attend to; the place where YOU are the one and only subject

SURROUNDINGS

Our Happy Home

Sick, twisted
Broken, so fix it
Mend it, no longer suspend it
For so long I've depended on our "happy home"

Love me despite of
Your feeling of no love
Take us above these moments of despair
Hold me, console me
Stop trying to mold me
No need to scold me
Just show me you care

You're hurting, I know it
Now and then you show it
I try to hold it, but I'm not the cause of your pain
Maybe we can be beyond what we see
Be a happy family
Bring each other out of the rain

You know me, I know you
Let's do better than what we do
So much ado
Don't wanna be alone
Let's try solutions for a conclusion
To all this confusion in our "happy home"

Maxine

I'm a crack addict
I get a hit every night
I have childrens, so maybe that'll make it right
Yeah, I have an apartment, but I'm forever in the streets
I have stolen diamonds in my head down to my feet
I don't need marriage because I'll just take a man's dough
If I get him drunk enough he'll neva know
My childrens share clothes and eat from same plate
Why waste food when da rent is 5 months late
I had childrens so welfare can pay my way
I don't love them but dey still betta do what I say
I had lovin' parents but then somethin' went wrong
When I told dem I believed at 14 I should be on my own
I stopped believing in God when my friend was shot down
So my parents chose to no longer have me around
I make money by selling my body
Hey, you gotta do what you have to do to make ends meet
Quickies make a person like me feel complete
Ev'body my friend even though dey talk about me
Talk is just talk it not reality
I had black eyes from 'busive guys
Who found out what I was about and chewed me out
I don't care about God's world or this life given to me
What I could've been remains a mystery
On television my story you've probably seen
Don't fo'get bout me
My name is Maxine

Secrets

Another thing to keep on your mind to remember not to tell, although it may cause pain for those you keep it from, or for those who leaked it to you. Eventually, you'll just end up telling another lie to your loved one.

Scarred

I don't want most of the good things that come to me
To be a serendipity
I want the opportunity to know that on my own I'm able to shine
My way through this mess of all this grief and stress
Doubters telling me that I am less has finally pushed me to the test
To accept that I'm partially, physically scarred

This domestic violence only secludes me in silence
Hollers of "bitch" and "whore" makes me wanna pack my shit and go
Runaway to a brighter day, though most problems follow me anyway,
But if here I continue to stay, I'll continue to be mentally scarred
By the things you do and this life that I go through
This dead pain inside I must let go because I'm no longer able to hide
This hurt of this thorn in my side
What others want me to do I cannot abide
Leaving me socially scarred

Childhood circumstances damn near blew my chances
To have the life that I want to live
I may not forget, maybe I'll forgive
I'm unable to be selfish, I choose to give
All that I have in this lifetime to lyrically express my mind
Of being emotionally scarred
Scarred temporarily
I don't have to stay down necessarily
I'm in control of my own destiny, so no need to feel insecurity
Each and every day I'm here breathing the sweat of this dismay
I'm going to be out there to succeed
Answering to my each and every need
No time to beg and plead, while I'm living here, sitting here, breathing here...

Scarred

Survive

I get up early in the morning time
without time to hear my woman whine.
I'm trying to be spiritually grown.
Besides, she told me she can make it on her own,
so I choose to stay gone.

I got somewhere I want to be,
so there's little time to respond to what's said about me.
I want to be continually blessed.
I guess it comes with the stress.
Why is my life such a mess?

My dad is still around.
He's not my perfect image, at least he's down
with the decisions I make out on the town
whenever I'm abound trying to reach higher ground.

If love is not enough, then what else is there?
Anyone can pretend that they care,
    but they're not with you having fun...
nothing is new under the sun.
I've achieved a new outlook on life that has nothing to do with strife.
I'm looking forward to the next day with all doubts put away
for good times will come my way.
As the world keeps turning, and I'm applying the lessons I'm learning
I'll continue to strive knowing that I'll … I will survive.

I Thank You Not

I thank you not for the vulgar language
I thank you not for the unnecessary changes
I thank you not and I'll be alright
Because the sun will shine at the end of my journey
Through the day my mind is unending
Due to all my thoughts I'm attending
Every emotion I express I can't be pretending
Yet, still, I have to wrap myself in my own concern
I have news to tell you, but you're years away
I don't have to waste time thinking of something positive to say
If expressions say it all, you shouldn't be threaten to look my way
I guess communication bear moments of pain
I thank you not for calling me out of my name
I thank you not for teaching me life is a deceitful game
However, I do want to thank you for showing me
I can be strong on my own, so *Thank You*

Bitch

That night on the streets for a little Trick or Treat
Little did I know later in life I would feel incomplete
The hurt that I thought would pass seemed to last
Since then, I never stopped wishing the same would happen to your ass
I've avoided most issues that knocked on my front door
Self-pity to me proved to be a bore
When it comes to judgment day,
I must admit I want to be there to hear what you have to say
I hope on earth you will know how it feels to cry from depression,
Feel like you're a burden on your loved one's impression,
Feel like someone has stolen your dreams,
And not be the star of the football team
In terms of walking, I which we could switch
You drunk, selfish, cold hearted BITCH

Dial Tone

Want a good time? Dial 1. Need a good laugh? Dial 2. Trying to reach a family member? Dial 3 and leave a message. Desire to feed your hunger? Dial 4 and hold on. Struggling to get the knife out of your back? Dial 5. Need a life? Dial 6. Need hot water? Dial 7. Got a prank call to report? Dial 8 or 9. Want to talk out your problems to a temporary ear? Dial 0.

Sperm Donor
from the lips of males of fatherless children

I didn't get this trait from my mother, so I must have gotten it from you
I'm tired of feeling guilty for the chaos we put each other through
Any man can donate sperm, so I guess you can call yourself a man
We're only human is what I taught myself to understand
Being human you have to reap what you sow
A child needs a lot in order to grow
I've received answers, but there's a lot I still don't know
However, I do know how to treat a woman right,
And not to go bed hopping whenever we get in a fight
I know to provide for my family, and put a roof over their head,
And tell my children they're not better off dead
If things don't work out like I want them to be
I'll be mindful to not let my children forget about me
I won't let them settle for I'll do what I can
I'll move hell and earth just to hold their hand
"I love you" won't be just a check in the mail,
Or a ten-page letter from behind the bars of jail
Childhood, adolescence, teenage crisis all look at the fact
That one sperm with a sense of direction
    is supposed to take care of all of that

LOVE'S SHADOWS

Woman

She doesn't need a king to be considered a queen,
But every now and then she allows a man to intervene
Into the things that are unseen
She's my other half, my chosen path,
My bread and butter who I'll trade for no other

She's not turned on by guys with pants hanging off their ass
Because she knows cheap thrills don't last
She doesn't call me her lazy nigga, or cast me into the river of
stereotypical minds
She takes me for who I am, and tell other females this man is mine
She respects a man with a job and who's trying to make it happen

She gives me good love, like whoa
She gives me good, well, you know, like whoa
She doesn't have false sensations
Nor is she a deadly temptation
When we meet there's a definitely a celebration
She's god fearing and not domineering

She has inner beauty and appeal
She a poetic flow like Jill Scott and Lauryn Hill
We chill in the breeze
Lay back and smoke a few trees
This woman isn't meant to be my slave
This woman isn't meant to degrade, then take half

This woman loves me
This woman loves me
This woman loves me
This woman loves me
She's not afraid to hold her head up high and be called a *Woman*

Somewhere Between Hello and Now

Somewhere between hello and now
I fell deep in love somehow
Love at first sight took over my mind
I'm so set on us spending time
Together and perhaps entertain the notion of forever
But, I'm living the here and now
And still pondering how I fell in love somehow

Oh, yeah I know why somehow
I fell in love somewhere between hello and now
You lent your ears, offered your heart, and said you wouldn't part
To an ordinary someone that wouldn't mean much,
But I'm not of this world for things I can only touch
Somewhere between hello and now
I heard "I love you" enough from you somehow
To know that your love is genuine and true
I'm unable to look in the mirror without thinking of you
Because somewhere, somehow I've learned to enjoy
Every moment we spend together now

Maybe Then

We don't talk and I'm lonely
It's hard to breathe when you're not with me
I think of you more than a time or 2
Just to keep myself from being blue
If you say to me that you'll remain faithfully
Then maybe, baby
I'll know that you'll be around to always keep me bound
About your daily, every situation

Let me know what's in your heart from the start
I'll do my best; we must remain strong
Honesty doesn't do us wrong
Believe in me then you'll see that my love is no mystery
Baby, then maybe, your insight will invite me into your loving arms
Your wisdom will ignite my soul
Then maybe we'll avoid becoming spiritually old
Baby, then maybe, the fire will inspire all that we desire
Understanding will start commanding this thing called Truth
Maybe then, baby

Why Do I Have Your Number Again

Why do I have your number again?
Apparently, it's for safe-keeping, and you call yourself a friend?
Sure, I can dial it and get your voice mail.
A voice machine is too weak to hear what I have to tell.
Maybe I'm supposed to call to see if you need anything.
I feel that you're under the telephone every time it rings,
but you don't pick up because you know it's me.
All I want is an answer as to why do I have your number again?
Why do I have your number again?
My phonebook will remain spacious,
my feelings will remain unheard to your ears.
Your 7 digits and area code are ashes to me.
I can't sit here dialing your number
    when there are other places I would rather be,
and when I think about it,
    if we came face to face I wouldn't know where to begin.
Come to think of it, why do I have your number again?

Whatever Happened To

Whatever happened to you loving me? Whatever happened to me loving you? We lost interest somewhere in yesterday's past. Forever was never promised, but who wants to think of the negative "could be"? Whatever happened to no more half-truths? Whatever happened to through sickness and health? Words can be so damn deceiving. Whatever happened to the trust? Whatever happened to us? With every 't' crossed, whatever happened to whatever we lost?

But That's a Separate Story

I think I know that person's desire, but that's a separate story.
If you want to burn keep adding fuel to the fire,
    but that's a separate story.
I keep to myself for a reason, but that's a separate story.
It all depends on the season, but that's a separate story.
I smile when I'm expected to cry, but that's a separate story.
Who really cares as to why? But, again, that's a separate story.

Let's get to the bottom of all this mess.
Focus on reality and cut the BS.
We can only pretend that the stories are not relating.
There's no need for all this speculating.
The fact that we're not communicating
makes it the same story heard over and over again!

Jelly

When I need you the most you're unavailable.
The last time I saw you I put you on the shelf.
Now, I need back my jelly to fill my joy and belly.
Your last spread had me feeling dread.
It was not your best performance.

I've tried other solutions, but there were no resolutions.
So, I'm back seeking the thrill of you.
Why do me the way you do?
Do you want to hear me plead that I need my jelly?
You're no ordinary jelly; you're my pudding pop.
Come back to me, baby, and put me back on top.

Jelly, you told me a secret, and you didn't panic if I would keep it.
I just want to go back to the way we were...someone please help me!
Take away this hurt! My jelly is gone!
If you find It please send It back home.

Black Roses

Mahogany, Dark, Ebony, and Tar
are changing the way things are or were this hour.
Here's something fresh that'll relieve stress off ya chest;
Black has laid to rest any obstacles of your unforeseen. So, stop
and recognize the beauty of the roses.

Kiss Me

I couldn't resist.
I had to insist, especially when you love me like this.
Come here
  Come closer
Here's a kiss from me to you

Just Because

Just because you can't break me
doesn't mean I'm made of stone.
Just because we don't communicate
doesn't mean I want to be alone.

Just because you have my heart
doesn't mean you can break it.
Just because you love me
doesn't give you the right to fake it.

Just because we disagree
doesn't mean it's not you I'm thinking of
Just because we're only human
doesn't mean we can't sincerely love

Starvation

@ the tip of my soul
melancholy lingers like an empty hollow.
I search for direction which I will refuse to follow;
too many misguided concerns persuaded me astray.
My soul is starved on this day.

I post on a wall.
Passersby I observe. I'm not allowed the alone time I yearn for, deserve.
Misconstrued words cover what I say.
My calmness is starved this day.

I live and breathe gospel, enjoying the knowledge of the Higher Being.
I'm not always excited by what's seen.
@ times I feel there should be more.
Human materialistic I cannot ignore.
I need to focus and remember to pray.
My spirit is starved this day.

People want to run over me, possibly want to control my mind.
They should live their life; I'm determined to live mine.
My stressing blocks My blessing.
Sometimes my concern has to be stern.
I'm suffering from starvation.
When will I ever learn?

Long Distance

You probably still love me, even though it's long distance love.
Hopefully, you care about me, even though it'll be long distance caring.
Maybe you'll acknowledge my existence, even though it'll be long
    distance knowledge.
Prayerfully, you'll pick up the telephone, even though it'll be a long
    distance call.
Respectfully, you're probably thinking of me, even though they're long
    distance thoughts.
Graciously, you'll still remember my face, even though it'll be a long
    distance remembrance.
You're probably trying to reach out to me, even though long distance
    has put a distance between us.
You may even trust me, even though I don't know much of you to trust.
Long distance has revealed the truth, and the fact that we don't
    communicate is the proof.
I guess I should apologize for my resistance, well, no I shouldn't
    because I'm not to blame for you being --------------------long
    distance

I Thought My Name Was

I thought my name was Love,
    but all you gave me was a reflection of hate.
I thought my name was Patience,
    but you made it your business to always be late.
I thought my name was Forgiveness,
    but forgiveness was never in your heart.
I thought my name was Caring,
    but you never cared about me from the start.
I thought my name was Honor,
    but you never could give credit where it was due.
I thought my name was Eternity,
    because that's how long I wanted to be with you.
I thought my name was Peace,
    but you only wanted to cuss and fight.
I thought my name was Honest,
    because that's the only way to make it right.
I thought my name was Reliable,
    because I couldn't depend on you.
I thought my name was Special,
    but that faded after all you put me through.
I'm not pointing fingers
    because I'm not blameless.
It's just disappointing to know until you get your act together,
    in your book I shall remain Nameless.

Vaseline

I don't need any Vaseline
I prefer my ash to be shown
I don't need to borrow your Vaseline
I can afford my own
I don't need your Vaseline
Physically, I've grown
I don't desire your Vaseline, so leave me alone

Don't give me your Vaseline
I can put my own smile on my face
I don't need to be associated with your Vaseline,
so I decide to stay in my own space
Your Vaseline is trifling. I can't use it anytime or anyplace
I have no love for your Vaseline
I know where to find my own embrace

I can do without your Vaseline
I can find another soul mate if I choose to connect
Your Vaseline is cold hearted, and surely I'll be a reject
I overlook your Vaseline
I can create my own shine
In my world your Vaseline doesn't exist, and mine has been redefined

See What Listening to Them Got You

See what listening to them got you...
Alone,
  Miserable,
    Feeling sorry for your actions.
You said you Trusted me,
      Loved me,
        Respected me,
         Cared about me,
but none of those things were shown
  when you took their words over mine.
They filled your head with lies,
    causing you to look the other way.
You never came to me to see if they were true.
  You just assumed and threw me to the side.
    Well, you found out they were lying a little too late,
because I'm with someone else giving her all that I was about to give
you
        and all that you wish you had.....

CONCLUSION

Overcome

I told you my story. I gave you my song, to inform, like me, you too can overcome.

Though the blade maybe sharp, and the hills maybe firm, you just have to keep moving forward, and take the lessons learned.

I told you my story. I gave you my song,
to inform, like me, you too can overcome.
There's going to be dangerous storms and snow.
Just remember the knowledge and experience that aids you
as you grow.

I told you my story. I gave you my song, to inform, like me, you too can overcome. The barriers that try to keep you from what you believe, or issues that keep you down and from what you can achieve.

I told you my story. I gave you my song,
to inform like me, you too can overcome. Dotted eyes and
crooked T's may flood the land, but you don't have to succumb
to them. Let your feet be the roots to where you Stand.

Respect where you come from
Rise like the sun
Believe in belief
and continue to overcome

The Ole Country Days

It was the fifth Sunday in October when I decided to visit the place that held my most favorable childhood memories. The white and green olive home still stood there vibrating light. The sunflower in the front garden was no longer standing erect, reaching towards the sky, but the home was still there. A vehicle wasn't parked at the side of the home like I always remembered, but I knew someone was inside. The two front steps were going to be a challenge because of my wheelchair. I just had to get inside the home, just had to hear the words of wisdom from the person that I knew was inside. I pushed my wheelchair up the driveway and then on to the side ramp. Then I shifted my weight on to the second stair. My legs were weak, however, I had great upper body strength. I grabbed the wheelchair by the foot rest and proceeded to pull the wheelchair up the stairs. The screen door slammed in a hurry once I got on the porch safely. I took a few minutes to catch my breath before shifting my weight back into the wheelchair. I made it. I was prepared to spend much needed quality time with one of my heroes. I was prepared for some grandpops and grandson time.

I opened the screen door leading into the home, and gave the wooden door one hard knock. I knew that it took time for him to get to the door, so I waited patiently. As I waited, a strong, autumn's wind blew. I love cooler weather. My hands trembled. I started to have thoughts of maybe I should've called first, but I never had to call first in the past because someone was always here. I saw someone peek through the living room curtains. The door opened. At that moment I felt my mission was half way accomplished.

"Heyyyyyyy, Elrow!" Grandpops said with a smile on his face. It always made my day better when he greeted me with a smile. I wondered where he got the name "Elrow" from, but since he called me that, I just figured it was his name for me.

"Hey, granddaddy!"

"Come on in here out that hawk!"

I loved how grandpops inserted his country lingo into our conversations. As I pushed through the front door into the living room I smelt the all familiar scent of lemon fresh Pine Sol, which meant grandpops still cleaned early in the morning. The antique, wooden clock on the wall read 8:35 a.m.. I followed grandpops into his bedroom where the television was located. The room was just how I remembered it. Grandma's recliner chair was located beside grandpop's recliner chair. I paused to have a brief, emotional moment. I knew grandma was in a better place, however, a little selfish part of me wanted her to be on earth a little while longer. I didn't allow grandpops to see me in my feelings. I whispered hello to grandma. Grandpops sat down in his chair.

"Who helped you up the steps dere, Elrow?" Grandpops asked like he already knew the answer.

"God gave me the strength."

"I know He did. You keep letting the Lord use you, and you gone be alright." Grandpops took a few sips of water from the glass he sat beside his chair then continued to speak. "Yeah, back in dem ole country days my folks didn't go to church on fifth Sundays because fifth Sundays were very rare."

Grandpops had shared this information with me before. It didn't bother me, though. We had a lot of catching up to do. I felt blessed to still have my grandpops in my life well into my mid twenties.

"I know you haven't ate yet, so come on in here and get you some breakfast."

Yep, just by the aroma I knew what was on the menu: fried chicken, grits, and biscuits. Of course, grandpops covered his two pieces of chicken with gravy and dared anyone to eat those pieces. He knew that I tried to remain as independent as possible, and didn't want anyone taking pity on me, so he sat the pots and pans where I could get to them easily. I parked at the left end of the kitchen table like I always had. Grandpops didn't eat at the table with me, which was alright. I looked at the other end of the table and saw grandma's spirit. She was smiling and drinking coffee. I smiled back and she disappeared.

After eating I pushed my wheelchair back into grandpops' room, and thanked him for the meal. He was watching television. On Sundays he kept the television tuned on ABC until around 1 p.m.. He liked looking at the news and George Stephanopoulos' show, *This Week*. I would've washed my plate. Grandpops never wanted me to, though. I started to open my mouth until I saw grandpops nod off.

I never witnessed grandpops be eccentric. In fact, I knew his daily schedule by heart. He woke up, prayed, and got out of bed at 3:45 a.m. every morning. I know because sometimes I spent the night on the living room couch. While he cleaned he listened to the gospel station on his clock radio. Once done with the cleaning he sat down for a minute to listen to the radio. By 5 a.m. no later than 5:30 he was at the stove preparing breakfast.

I didn't want to make the slightest noise to disturb him, so I rolled myself on to the screened in porch. The wind had calmed down. I could still tell it was autumn, though with the pine cone and dried honeysuckle scent in the air from the front yard. During the summertime visits the porch provided relief from the heat of the house that the window fans could not provide. I sat on the green swing grandpops hand built. I rocked back and forth recalling the different games my cousins and I created when we were younger. Grandma's spirit appeared again. This time she was sitting on a stool making dolls. She was very creative in doll making and baking cakes. I never bothered over when these visions of her would stop. Honestly, I didn't want them to. On any other Sunday family members would come over after church, however, on this particular Sunday grandpops and I had the environment to ourselves. I decided to go back to the bedroom to continue our visit together.

I rolled in on him still taking a catnap. Out of nowhere I heard him speak.

"Back in dem ole country days we had to make sure we prayed. Having such a big family I didn't know how we were going to make it sometimes, but the Lord always made a way. I got paid pennies on the dollar working out in the fields with that ole mule in the hot sun. We always had exactly what we needed. We never tried to live beyond our means. Yeah, the Lord provided ALL we needed."

Whenever I heard grandpops say "back in dem ole country days" I grabbed my mental notepad. I didn't know if he knew it or not, but grandpops ALWAYS spoke to my current situations indirectly, or quite possibly directly. He grabbed his VCR remote and switched on a movie. It was a videotape of grandma! One of my uncles was holding the video camera filming grandma in her "heaven", her vegetable garden. I couldn't tell if she was gathering collards or peas. I wasn't paying that much attention to what she was gathering. I just loved hearing her voice one more time. She had on one of house dresses. I thought grandpops would be in tears. I looked in his direction, and he was smiling and laughing with his pearly white teeth. I misjudged that one totally.

"There she is. Look at Fan!" Grandpops said through laughter. He must have been thinking of grandma, too, like I was earlier.

By 1 p.m. grandpops told me to go to the kitchen table and eat. This time he fixed my plate. Since it was Sunday I knew he cooked some kind of greens whether it be collards, turnips, or mustard greens. This day he cooked collards, hen, butter beans, and cornbread. He said he was going to eat later, closer to the time for him to take his medication. I always viewed him as a healthy man, so I wondered what kind of medication he was taking, but I digressed.

"I'm proud of you, Elrow." I tried to shy away from any admiration or praise thrown in my direction. "You have the odds stacked against you, and you keep going. The Lord kept you here for a reason. You're going to make it because you're my grandson. God has not forgotten. Noooooooo, He ain't forgot. He still the same today like He was yesterday, like He will be tomorrow."

It never crossed my mind that grandpops loved any of his other grandsons more than I. Him taking ownership of me as his grandson pleased my ears, grabbed my heart. I almost kicked myself because we never spoke like this in earlier years. I thought he was mute, or just didn't like talking. He told me once that everything happens in God's timing, so I stopped being so hard on myself.

"Have you talked to any of your aunts or uncles?" Grandpops asked.

"No, not recently."

Grandpops handed me his cell phone. It still shocked me that he decided to get one finally. "Here Elrow. Make sure I got everyone number I'm supposed to have in dere."

I put on my thinking cap and recalled everyone from his eldest child to his youngest great, great grandchild. I didn't mind at all. This was our quality time together. After I finished programming the numbers, he called some of the relatives and asked about their well being.

Although I hated to depart, I had to get home because I didn't want to travel by myself in the dark, and since it was daylight savings time, I decided to leave at 3:45 p.m.. That gave me enough time to make it home by 5 before it got dark.

"Alright granddaddy I'm about to go home before it get dark. Thank you for everything. I really enjoyed myself."

"Alrighttttttt then, Elrow! Come back to see me when you can."

Grandpops never ceased to amaze me when he told me to come back when I could and not if I could.

The telephone rang. I rushed through my front door to answer. It was one of my cousins saying that I needed to get down to the hospital with grandpops because he was down there by himself. Hospital??? I hadn't heard any recent news about him being sick. I paused and recalled the last few visits I had with him. He spoke to me like he was giving me an overview of his life like he was saying goodbye. I received this phone call right in the afternoon heat of a summer's day. That didn't matter. I switched over to my power wheelchair and left for South Fulton Hospital.

I arrived at the hospital within a 30 minute time window from receiving the phone call. The receptionist at the desk told me his room number, but all I heard was the end of the hallway. The closer I got to his room, the further his room seemed. It almost felt like I was traveling a long, dark stretch of hell. I wasn't ready to say goodbye to my hero. He was my only surviving grandparent. He was the only non judgmental person remaining in my life. He was the only one who would listen first before giving me advice. He was one of few who knew my love is genuine.

Finally, I had reached his room. I was misinformed. His room was standing room only with my mother, aunts, uncles, and some of my cousins. I spoke to them then looked at grandpops. He was heavily sedated. I grabbed his left hand and told him I was there for him. The cancer had spread. Doctors came in and pulled members of the family in the hallway to discuss how long grandpops had left on earth. I looked in grandpops direction and told him not to leave me yet. A cousin and I were the last ones to leave him. I told him I'll return the next day.

Grandpops must have heard me because the nursing staff said that someone from the family had to sit with him at night because he was unruly and abusive towards them. No, I didn't condone his behavior, however, it did me good to hear that he still had fight in him. Furthermore, I did not think the staff was lying because he never liked anyone taking care of him or picking up after him. Since I was used to spending days and/or nights with him at home, I volunteered to stay with him at the hospital. The family made sure I was equipped with money and food, and they left us alone. I wasn't afraid or fearful. I knew it was time for me to be there for him like all those countless times he was there for me.

I heard him mumble every once and a while. Sometimes he spoke clearly.

"Elrow, I want to go home. Elrow, I want to go home." he repeated.

"Ok, granddaddy we're going to go home real soon." I knew that there wasn't a chance of him going back to 511 Third Avenue, so I made his hospital room feel like home. I turned the television to the Atlanta Braves game. Then I put the remote control in his hospital gown pocket, because he always kept the remote in his shirt pocket at home. I located his baseball cap and put it on his head.

He wasn't allowed to have any food, which I viewed as torture. I couldn't grasp that doctors had done all they could do. I started singing:

> *Sit down servant, sit down*
> *Sit down servant, sit down*
> *Sit down servant, sit down*
> *Sit down and rest a little while*

"Good stuff, Elrow. Good stuff" Grandpops interrupted. I continued while tears started running down my cheeks. I grabbed his left hand and promised him I was going to be alright.

Grandpops was doing fine. He had remained calm and peaceful up until 2 a.m.. When I started to get sleepy is when he decided to have a lot of energy, which baffled me because he was on such a high dosage of medication. He got out of the bed and was actually standing on his own two feet!

"Elrow, let's go home!"

"Granddaddy, we have to wait until the bus starts running." I said in my most comforting voice. "I promise we're going to get out of here." I had no clue how we were going to break out of there. I knew in my heart it was time for him to claim his resting place. I just wanted him to leave inside 511 Third Avenue.

A nurse walked in and told us it was important he stay in bed. She hooked him back up to the machines. Grandpops grabbed her wrist. She looked over at me frightened.

"Granddaddy, this is Elrow! I'm here with you!" He loosened his grip, and that made me feel better. Although the early morning hours were challenging, I was glad that he still knew who I was, that hearing my voice eased him.

I didn't ask for an extra bed. I slept in my power wheelchair. Yes, I was very uncomfortable, but that was my grandfather. This was my chance to be there for him like he was there for me.

"Elrow, I gotta pee!" He started getting out of the bed again. I never heard him speak like this or utter a cuss word before.

"Granddaddy, stay in the bed. I'll get a nurse."

I rolled into the hallway to the nurses' desk. I told them grandpops needed help getting to the restroom. My ears were not prepared for the response, "tell him to go in his diaper." Before I knew it I told the nurse to go in her diaper. I thought that was very demeaning for the nurse to suggest I tell him to urinate in the diaper they had placed on him. I returned to the room. I was not about to tell him what the nurse said, so I rolled to the toilet located inside his room, and picked up the urinal.

"Here you go granddaddy. Your legs are a little too weak to walk right now, so you have to use this. I turned my head and rolled back towards the room entrance. Once he was done I placed the urinal beside his bed. About 30 minutes later a nurse and tech came into the room with supplies to change him.

"Excuse me sir. I thought you said he had to urinate." Both of them said as they discovered that he did not urinate in the diaper.

"I was not about to tell him to "use it" in a diaper! He used the urinal, so what's the damn problem?!" At this point I didn't care who I offended, who reported me, who didn't like my tone on the hospital staff.

Although his sheets and gown were not dirty, they changed the bed and grandpops then left the room.

The doctor came in at 8 'o' clock the next morning. I acted as a representative for the family, which meant I had to tell them the news I'm sure most of them already knew. He was being taken off the machines, and we had to decide what was the best possible care for him during his final hours. I had accepted that he was leaving. I just didn't want him to be put in a hospice. To me, hospice meant they were killing him. I was told he would be comfortable at a hospice. Grandpops told me over and over again that we're not in this world for comfort. The good Lord gave us strength to be warriors, and we were meant to fight.

Once enough of the family members got there I told them the news. I refused to argue that I didn't want him to go to a hospice, so I compromised. I had to be there with him. One of my aunts told me to go home and get some rest. I admitted that I needed a haircut, a shower, and a good eight hours sleep. That day was Friday. I rolled back into his hospital room and told him that I would return Sunday after church, and we would watch the Atlanta Braves game on TBS.

"I'm going home on the morning train. I'm going home on the morning train. The evening train maybe too late. I'm going home on the morning train." I never heard him sing this song, however, this was his reality. Just like he woke up around 3:45 a.m. every morning, he answered God's call early Sunday morning. I was asked to welcome the visitors at church that morning. I wanted to shut down. Grandpops wouldn't like that at all, though. I welcomed the guests at church like I knew God and family welcomed him into eternal rest.

Grandpops instilled in me morals, wisdom, and most of all, loving beyond measures. He taught me a lot and told me things that I'll take with me to the grave. Not one day that goes by that I don't think about the ole country days.